I Have a Right
to See Him. . . .

I kept staring at the picture of my father, hoping it would tell me something. Peggy would say he was gorgeous. But he couldn't be my father. I had always thought that when I saw him I'd know. I thought I'd *feel* we were related. But I didn't feel anything. I could have been looking at a picture in a magazine.

Mom was looking at me anxiously. "So, do you feel better now that you've seen him? You can see how young we were. . . ."

"Yeah." I didn't want to talk to her about him. I was angry that I didn't feel anything, angry that my own father was a total stranger to me. I didn't care if she thought she had done the right thing. I was angry with her because of what she had done, right or wrong.

But I wasn't uncertain anymore about what I had to do. I knew I had to see him, and I had to see him soon. . . .

Tell Me No Lies

Hila Colman

AN ARCHWAY PAPERBACK
POCKET BOOKS • NEW YORK

POCKET BOOKS, a Simon & Schuster division of
GULF & WESTERN CORPORATION
1230 Avenue of the Americas, New York, N.Y. 10020

Published by arrangement with Crown Publishers, Inc.
Library of Congress Catalog Card Number: 78-1285

ISBN: 0-671-29920-4

First Pocket Books printing September, 1980

10 9 8 7 6 5 4 3 2 1

AN ARCHWAY PAPERBACK and ARCH are trademarks
of Simon & Schuster.

Printed in the U.S.A.

Chapter One

Mom and I were in her bedroom talking about Larry Brandon, the guy she was going to marry. "He is not going to adopt me," I shouted. I pushed my fist into the pile of clothes on her bed where I was sitting.

"All right, all right," she said, obviously not meaning it. "But I wish I knew why. You say you like him, and he's crazy about you." She held up a black lacy thing to show me. "See, I'm throwing all these old slips away. They're too short anyway. Isn't that good of me?"

"Terrific," I said. She never throws anything away. She must have clothes from the year one. Her room is always a mess, and I never could understand how she managed to get herself dressed and to work on time. She always looked good too. But I wasn't going to let her change the subject. "You know why. By the way, when you married my father did you have a wedding?"

"We just went down to City Hall. Look at this nightgown. I bought it before you were born. It's torn, but I can fix it. . . ."

"Was it part of your trousseau?" I asked.

Mom put down the gown and looked at me. "No, Angela, I did not have a trousseau. Why do we have to go through this again?"

"Because it's not finished. You never tell me *anything* about my father. You never want to talk about him." I was shouting again.

"You're right. I don't want to talk about him. I've told you all I can. I was barely eighteen when I married him. My parents had just been killed in an

4

accident, I was alone—I thought I loved
him. We got married, and soon after
you were born he got a good offer for a
job in Saudi Arabia. I was afraid to go
there with a tiny baby, so I stayed
home. He never came back and we got
divorced. Now you know all that I
know."

"But I don't. I don't know anything
about him. I don't know things other
kids do. . . . Sally Brooke's parents are
divorced but she knows a lot about her
father. I've never even seen a picture
of *my* father. . . ."

Mom sat down on the bed beside me.
"Darling, can't you forget about him?
Larry wants to be your father, he wants
to adopt you—your father isn't a real
person for me anymore and he can't be
for you. Don't make yourself miserable. . . ."

But I was miserable. She didn't understand. No one understood. It had nothing
to do with Larry, except that their getting married and his wanting to adopt
me brought everything to the surface.
When I was younger, I hadn't thought
about my father so much, except when

5

things came up like the father-and-daughter dinner at school. I wasn't going to go and I told myself that I didn't care. But then Dr. Levine, my best friend Peggy's father, called me up and invited me. I hate people to feel sorry for me.

I'm almost thirteen years old and I know how to take care of myself. I've known how for a long time, because my mother has always worked. Until Larry came along, we often counted pennies until Mom got her paycheck. And I'm not stupid. I know that if a kid has never heard from her father, not even at Christmas and on birthdays, there's got to be something wrong. Either he's a bum, or something's wrong. It was not knowing what was wrong that made me uncomfortable. But I was determined to find out. No one wants to think of her father as a bum. Even my friend Tim, whose father really is a bum—although Tim doesn't like to admit it. He doesn't talk about it, but I know his father sometimes beats him up. But he acts like his father is super if he takes him to Yankee Stadium once in a blue moon.

Mom and I are close. We discuss money and stuff that most kids don't even know about, because their two parents work it out between them. But whenever I ask about my father, Mom clams up, and we are at war. I wasn't just being curious. I *needed* to know. I think kids have a right to ask questions and get answers. It's rotten not knowing where you came from, who you really are. I'm like a nothing, I could have come out of a bottle.

"You do like Larry, don't you?" Mom asked for the tenth time.

I nodded yes. I did like Larry. He doesn't treat me like a baby, the way some of Mom's friends do. They're always asking me if I'm afraid to be alone in the house or if I'm afraid to go shopping by myself. Larry trusts me. He's also a good cook, which is more than I can say for my mother. She forgets to shop and would eat hot dogs and TV dinners every night if you'd let her. Larry makes things that take a long time to cook and he uses all kinds of herbs and spices.

But I did not want him to adopt me. Right or wrong, I felt that would be the end of ever finding out anything about my father. One thing I had never told my mother was that when I was old enough, I was going to go to Saudi Arabia to look for him. And no one was going to stop me.

The morning of the wedding Mom woke up looking awful. She said she felt sick and was nervous. "You got married before, you ought to be used to it," I told her. I was having breakfast but all she wanted was a cup of tea.

"That was different," she said. "Besides, I wish you'd stop harping on that. I thought only old people lived in the past."

"Then I'm old. Do I have to wear that dress you bought?" It was a ridiculous long dress and I hated it, but Mom had her heart set on it, so in the store I agreed to wear it. But now I couldn't stand the thought of putting it on.

"Yes, of course. Angela, what'll I do

with my hair? It looks awful. I never should have had it tinted. Larry will hate it."

"I told you not to. But it looks okay. Want some toast?"

"No, thank you. Angie, I'm so nervous. Do you think there's enough ice for the champagne? What time is it? The caterer should be here soon. . . ."

"Relax. You're only getting married to Larry after all. You've been practically living with him for a year so what's the big deal?"

"Oh, dear, you shouldn't talk that way." I think she really blushed. "It's funny but getting married *is* different. I feel like a bride."

I roared. "Maybe I should tell you the facts of life, all about the birds and the bees. It's like this, Mom . . ."

She had to laugh too. "I'm sure you know more than I do, but I'd just as soon not hear it. You know what? I really love him. I can't believe I feel the way I do at my age. I've never felt this way before."

Suddenly I felt sad. I wasn't going to talk about my father, I wasn't going to spoil her wedding day, but hadn't she loved him? Sometimes she said she had and other times she said she didn't know what love was about then. That was my mom, full of contradictions, especially about my father, one day saying he was terrible to have left her when I was a tiny baby, and the next saying she had been glad to be rid of him.

I felt cut off from her, left out. I felt sad and jealous, jealous that she loved Larry and hadn't loved my father the same way. It wasn't that I was jealous of Larry; I was just unhappy that she said this was the first time she was in love.

I put on the stupid dress, and actually with shoes instead of sneakers it didn't look so bad. Brushing my hair helped too. At least I had a full-length mirror now and could see what I looked like.

One thing I was thankful to Larry for was my room. On account of him, Mom and I had moved out of the tiny apartment we had, into this much larger place on Riverside Drive. I had a bedroom of sorts in our old apartment, but it was so small and narrow I couldn't even have a desk. Mom slept in the living room but she kept her clothes in my room, so it wasn't a real room of my own. Now I had everything, a big bed, lots of drawer space, a marvelous desk, closets of my own, and best of all, a private place where I could close the door and hang out a sign, DON'T COME IN. And I did, too, lots of times. And I didn't have Mom's mess all over the place. Mom said I was acquiring my own mess, but I thought my room was neat. I had a shell and rock collection but at least it was on a shelf, and lots of posters, and a couple of ratty fur rugs, and all my old dolls that used to have to be kept in a box. They were one thing I wouldn't throw out. I knew I was old for dolls and it was silly, but I thought they'd *feel* it.

I also had a big picture of Tim in my room, but only because it was so funny. He's very skinny—I don't think he eats enough because his mother's a vegetarian. I'm always bringing him meat sandwiches to school, especially corned beef, which he loves. The picture was taken when he went to Disneyland. Tim's skinny face was peering above the body of a fat man. It made me laugh every time I looked at it. Peggy said he was the homeliest boy in school, but I think she's a tiny bit jealous because I like him so much. Larry keeps teasing me about him. He thinks Tim is my boyfriend, which is about as far from the truth as you can get. I'm too young to have a boyfriend, and it couldn't possibly be Tim because there's nothing romantic about him. Mom thinks I'm more practical than romantic, but she doesn't know, and besides I don't see why you can't be both.

The caterers arrived and I had to show them where everything was because Mom was answering the phone and arranging flowers and running around being her usual disorganized self. She may be a good designer but she can do the nuttiest things. Like pouring orange juice into her coffee instead of milk or putting the mail in the fridge. Once she tore up an envelope with a fifty-dollar check in it.

Hordes of people came. Many of them

I had never seen before, Larry's friends and business friends of Mom's. We have no family. That's one reason Mom was into this adoption bit. She said that if anything happened to her I haven't a relative in the world. That made me mad. I did have a father someplace. But she was right that there was no one else. She was an only child, and I haven't any sisters or brothers. Larry has a mother and a brother, but they're in California and didn't come. I was introduced to a lot of people, but I don't remember any of their names.

Peggy had been invited, but it was Christmas vacation and she was away with her folks. I felt very guilty because I kept thinking about my own father, Robert Grey. It was weird; Mom and Larry looking all glowy and there I was thinking how it had been when they—Mom and my father—had gotten married. It made me feel terrible.

I was Mom's maid of honor, and standing beside her during the ceremony I had all I could do to keep from crying. I thought you'd have to love someone a lot to make all those prom-

13

ises. I just didn't understand how anyone could get divorced after saying those things in front of everyone, swearing to them before God. How could Mom really want to forget all about my father?

After the ceremony I wanted to be alone, so I took a plate full of food to my room. I was munching away, half listening to all the noise in the rest of the apartment, when I heard Larry call, "Hey, Mrs. Brandon, come over here."

Maybe I am stupid, but I hadn't thought about Mom's becoming Mrs. Lawrence Brandon. She had never used her married name before, but had just stayed Karen Dunoway. She said she had started out that way in business and didn't want to change. So after my father left she called me Angela Dunoway because she said it was easier for us both to have the same name. But now our names were going to be different, and it was dumb for me to be Angela Dunoway when my real name was Angela Grey. After this wedding was over and things settled down, I would tell Mom that I wanted to change my name.

Everything was going to be different now, not only our names. Larry had been in and out of our apartment a lot in the past year, but now he'd be part of the household. It was going to be odd to have a man in the house. In the past Mom used to say that it was kind of great *not* to have a man around. We would eat when we wanted to and what we wanted, and we didn't have any man trying to boss us or expecting to be waited on and taken care of. She said that most men were big babies and were spoiled, but she seems to have forgotten all the things she's said.

I was thinking about all this when she came in. She looked terrific in her brown chiffon dress, and her eyes were very blue and bright. "Angie, I couldn't imagine where you'd disappeared to. What are you doing in here by yourself?"

"Eating."

Mom laughed. "But why alone?"

"I just felt like it."

15

Mom's face clouded over. "Don't be sad, please don't be sad. It's going to be good to have Larry here. Nothing's going to be different between us."

"I'm okay."

"Then come on out. I want you to meet a very old friend of mine. She came down from the Cape just for this."

I gulped down the rest of my food and followed Mom back into the living room. Mom introduced me to a Miss Margaret Lathrop. She looked different from Mom's other friends—older and not stylish. I bet she never used makeup in her life. She was big and comfortable, and she was kind of shaped like a tent. She looked like someone who stayed out-of-doors in all weather and wasn't afraid to get her hair wet. I liked her. Mom said later that she wasn't as old as she looked. Anyway she didn't say dumb things to me. She told me about Provincetown, where she lived and had a shop and made jewelry. She was wearing some of it, silver bracelets and long dangling earrings. She had a wonderful ring that wound all the way up to the knuckle of her finger. She knew a lot about music—and all about the new bands and records, and classical music too. I was shy about asking questions but I think maybe she had been a musician once. She asked me to visit her in Provincetown sometime. I said I might, that it sounded like fun.

I don't know how late people stayed. The noise continued for a long time after I went to bed. I had pulled my bed next to the window so that I could see the lights in New Jersey across the river whenever I opened my eyes. Somehow they made me feel better.

Chapter Two

Something is going on in this house that I don't like. Nothing I can put my finger on, but funny looks between Mom and Larry and a feeling that they're talking about me when I'm not there. There's a sudden silence when I come into a room.

Larry's been here a few weeks but I'm not at all used to him. Yesterday I forgot and came out into the hall in my underwear and ran right into him. Larry laughed and said he'd seen naked girls before, but I didn't like it.

But that's not the important thing. I

finally got up my courage and announced last night at dinner that I was going to change my name from Dunoway to Grey. It was like dropping a bomb. Mom got very uptight. I could tell by her face, because she didn't say much. She looked like someone had hit her. Larry kept looking at her in an odd, funny way. He did say that he thought it would be foolish for me to change my name since everyone in school already knew me as Dunoway. "You should wait until you get older and see how you feel about it then," he said. "I'm hoping you'll change it to Brandon." Fat chance of that, I thought.

I didn't think it was any of his business, and I wished I'd waited until Mom and I were alone. But I didn't have much chance to be alone with Mom these days. Larry was always around. I wasn't rushing to make him a true member of the family, someone I could discuss my feelings with. I might have known he would bring up the adoption business again.

And I was right. The next night he came home with two new records for me. He is generous and always buying presents for Mom and for me, but sometimes I feel funny taking them. I'm worried that he wants something from me that I can't give him.

At dinner that night Larry said that since he was now married he was changing his will and of course he was taking care of me. "And outside of my feelings for you," he said, "it will be much more practical and very much in your interest if you agree to an adoption. My lawyer feels strongly about it. It is really for your protection—none of us understands why you object so much."

"Because someday I intend to find my own father, and I don't want to have an adopted one," I said.

Mom was stunned. "But you couldn't possibly. You could never find him. That's the craziest thing I ever heard of."

"It's not crazy," I said. "I'll find him. Other people do. I've read about people finding their parents when they're grown up. I will, and you won't be able to stop me."

Larry looked from Mom to me and shook his head. Finally he said, "I'm afraid it's not up to me, Karen. You know what I think and if I had any doubts before, I'm sure of it now. You're the one who has to do the talking."

Mom seemed close to crying.

"Think about it, Karen," Larry said. "You know I'm right."

"Right about what?" I asked.

"Nothing," Mom mumbled. "Forget it."

"Forget what? I'm not going to forget my own father. You two can forget about this adoption business. That's what needs to be forgotten." I was yelling again. "And what does Mom have to talk about?" I demanded.

Larry looked at Mom, but she just kept shaking her head, and then she burst into tears. In a second Larry had his arms around her. "Take it easy, hon. It's the only way; believe me, you'll feel a million times better. Just tell her the truth, that's all."

"What truth? What are you two hiding from me?" I was really scared. I was sure I was going to hear something awful.

"Take it easy, Angie," Larry said. "Your mother has something to tell you. Just be patient."

"I don't want to be paient. If you don't tell me I'm going to scream. I'll scream so loud they'll hear me in Yonkers."

"That won't do any good," Mom said, wiping her face with a tissue. She was pulling herself together, but her face looked grim. "Let's finish our dinner and talk later."

"I don't want to finish my dinner," I said.

Larry got up from the table. "I'll go out for a walk while you two have a talk."

Mom looked at him like he was her last friend. "But you haven't had your dessert."

"I'll get a cup of coffee on Broadway. Take it easy, honey."

After Larry left, Mom and I sat looking at each other for several minutes. She was twisting a strand of hair around her finger. "Why don't we get comfortable." She pushed her chair away from the table and got up. I followed her into the living room where we settled at either end of the sofa. She looked awful.

"Please stop playing games with me. Tell me the truth."

"I don't know how to begin. I should have told you he was dead . . . I wanted to a long time ago, but I didn't, and then later I was afraid it would upset you too much. . . ."

She sounded confused, and what she said wasn't registering. "Is he dead? Is my father dead?"

"No, he's not. The father you think about doesn't exist. He isn't real. I made him up." Now she was looking straight at me and speaking firmly.

"I don't know what you're talking about."

"Robert Grey doesn't exist. He's a fictitious character. I was never married, never divorced. Your father is someone else entirely. I made up Robert Grey."

I couldn't believe it. What she was saying didn't make sense. "That's crazy. You can't make up a person. You told me a million times Robert Grey is my father."

"But it's not true. He's not your father. He's nobody's father. I made him up." She was almost yelling at me.

I stared at her. She was my mother and she was telling me something that I had to understand, but I couldn't. No one can make up a father. I guess I must have looked pretty stupid because she said, "Angie, please understand. I lied to you. Robert Grey was a big lie."

I had been looking away and now I stared at her. She winced. "Don't look at me that way. Please. Come here, come and sit close to me."

I didn't move. When she stretched out her arms I turned and said, "Don't touch me. Just leave me alone."

She began to cry. "Say something. Yell at me, do something."

"There is no Robert Grey," I finally said. "I have no father."

"Of course you have a father. I'll tell you about him. I'll tell you the whole story."

I pulled farther away from her. "I

don't want to hear another of your made-up stories. I don't want to hear anything." I got up and ran into my room. If I'd had a lock on my door I would have locked it. I fell down on my bed, but I didn't cry. I couldn't believe that all the time she'd been lying to me. She didn't know anything that went on in my head: all the times I'd wondered about what my father was doing, what he looked like, if he ever thought of me. I imagined a million different things I'd say to him when I found him. *And she had made him up.* I felt stupid. She had humiliated me, treated me like an idiot.

And now I was trapped. Trapped with her and Larry. I was never ever going to be able to trust either one of them again.

Mom came into my room. She had stopped crying, but she looked miserable. I didn't care. I was glad. I wanted to hurt her. I hated her. I buried my face in my pillow because I didn't want to look at her.

She sat down on my bed and touched the back of my head.

"Go away and leave me alone."

"I'm not going to leave you alone. You've got to listen to me, even if you don't want to. It's important. I want to tell you about your father."

"I don't care about my father, or my mother either. I'm going to leave here the first minute I can. I'm only staying until I can figure out where to go."

"Angela, you've got to listen." She pulled me around and up. "Later we can talk about what you want to do. You've got to listen first."

"You're wasting your breath because I'm not going to believe a word you say."

"All right, don't believe me." She almost smiled, and I hated her smiling. "Just listen. Your father is a Portuguese fisherman. His name is José Avillar. It's a very simple story. I met him up in Provincetown the summer after my parents were killed. We fell in love—in those days it was called an affair. It was a summer romance. From the beginning we both knew getting married would be a mistake. So at the end of the summer we said good-bye. . . ." Her voice trailed off.

I put my hands over my ears. "I don't want to hear it. I'm not listening. Go away."

"You're being hateful."

"You're right," I yelled. "And I want to be."

"You're not making this any easier."

"Why should I? What happened? Does your conscience suddenly bother you?"

"I'm not going to answer that. I'm going to finish what we started. When I got back to New York I discovered I was pregnant. With you. Margaret, whom you met at the wedding, came down to New York. She was my only friend. We discussed it for a long time and we both agreed there was no point in telling José."

I was stunned. "You mean that my so-called father doesn't even know I exist." I was furious.

"I'm afraid that's right." She spoke hesitatingly. "It wasn't an easy decision. I knew I was taking on a big responsibility not telling him, not telling you, but I thought I was doing the right thing. I still think so. If he had known, he'd have wanted to get married. I

30

didn't want to marry him. It would have been a disaster. And then I was afraid they'd take you away from me if I refused. The Avillars are a strong family. His mother wanted him to marry a Catholic; she'd have wanted to bring you up Catholic. She had no use for me. To her I was another tourist, and all tourists were arrogant New Yorkers as far as she was concerned. She hated them. She would have made José fight, go to court."

"Weren't you in love with him?" The whole story was making me feel worse and worse.

She kept fussing with my bedspread, making little pleats in it and smoothing them out. "I guess I thought I was. But not deep down. It was more of an infatuation. We had so little in common."

"Except sex," I said coldly.

She glanced at me and looked away. "Okay, have it your way."

"Okay. So my father's a Portuguese fisherman. Big deal."

"I thought you'd be glad to know."

"Is that why you took almost thirteen years to tell me?"

Mom got up and walked over to the window. She spoke without turning around. "I never thought it would be this way. Maybe I never should have told you the truth."

"What did you expect? That I wasn't going to care that you lied to me, that you never trusted me enough to tell me the truth—that is, if this is the truth? Why'd you make up Robert Grey anyway? And where did you get that name from?"

"I made him up in the hospital. On the day you were born, there was no sun, just gray clouds outside. I didn't want anyone to track down José. After that, it was easy to just go on with it. I guess I was afraid if you knew you'd . . ."

"I'd what?" I knew what, but I wanted her to say it.

"That you'd want to go find him. Saudi Arabia was far away."

"But Provincetown isn't. Is he still there?"

"Margaret told me he's married. He has a wife and three kids. And his own fishing boat. He still makes his living fishing."

I was silent for a long time. It wasn't easy to give up Robert Grey. Or to feel the way I now did about Mom. To think that she'd made him up and named him after a cloudy sky. It was too much. I felt I had lost her along with Robert Grey. And I couldn't truly believe in José Avillar. He sounded like someone else made up. Even if he was true, I resented him.

"Did he ask you to marry him?"

"Yes and no. He asked me to stay in Provincetown with some idea of getting married eventually, but he didn't press it very hard. He knew as well as I that it wouldn't work. We were young but not crazy—there were too many things against us. Our background, our interests, his religion. I didn't want to be home alone while he was away fishing for weeks at a time. He was pretty macho, too, except with his mother. She bossed him."

"Doesn't sound like you cared about him," I said. "Robert Grey was a better story."

"This is *not* a story. This is the truth." Mom's eyes were flashing. She was an-

gry. "And stop being such a smart ass.
I made one mistake. I'm sorry. But
you're not to punish me forever."

"I'm not punishing you. I just don't
believe you."

We were still arguing when Larry
came back. I wanted her to shut up and
me to shut up, but we didn't. Larry took
one look at us and said that we had both
better calm down. "She won't believe
me," Mom said.

"I think that was to be expected.
Where's that picture you have of Avillar?"

"I don't know. I packed it someplace
when we moved. . . ."

"Find it. And her birth certificate.
You must have that somewhere too."

"I suppose I have. I don't know if I
can find it."

"I'll help you." Larry was being Big
Daddy trying to get everything solved
one, two, three. He didn't understand
how deep the rift was between Mom
and me. I guess he couldn't, since he
hadn't been there while we were arguing.

"It's ridiculous to have to prove to my

34

own daughter that I'm telling her the truth. To have to show her her birth certificate." Mom was still angry.

"But you did lie to her," Larry said quietly.

"I made up a story because I thought it would be easier for her. It's not such a crime."

"You make it sound like nothing," I yelled. "It wasn't just a story, like making up something that happened when I was a baby. You made up a story about *my father*. Not your father, *my* father. I think that's pretty important. *You* decided that I should grow up without a father, that I shouldn't know him, that he shouldn't even know I was born. That's a heck of a lot for you to decide." I was getting furious all over again.

"I thought I did the right thing, and I still think so." Mom spoke firmly, but her eyes were looking at me like she was asking me to forgive her. I looked away.

Larry took her arm and led her out of the room. I could hear them in the next room dumping stuff out of her desk.

Then I got even madder. I couldn't believe that all these years there had been a picture of my father in our house and I had never seen it. All the times I'd asked Mom what Robert Grey looked like and how come she didn't have a picture! I had a vision of Mom and Larry sitting on the sofa together talking about José Avillar while I'd been thinking of Robert Grey. How sneaky could they be!

Now I didn't want to see it. I went out in the hall, got my coat from the rack, and walked out of the house.

I headed for the stairs in case they heard me. I didn't want to be caught waiting for the elevator. I ran down the seven flights of stairs, and in a few minutes I was out on the street. It was a cold, windy evening and Riverside Drive was deserted. I walked up to Broadway where there were people and lights. Then I just walked. I had no plan, and I wasn't running away. I just wanted to think.

Chapter Three

You can't make up your mind to think. Thoughts start running wild, and all kinds of ideas pop into your head. In spite of the cold there were people walking on Broadway. I guess there always are. They made me lonesome, and I wondered what I was doing walking by myself in the cold when it was already dark. I thought of all the cozy evenings Mom and I had spent in our old apartment. It all seemed very long ago. In one evening everything had been shattered. I could never feel the same way about Mom again.

I didn't know which was worse, the lying or the final truth. I'm no goody-goody. I have lied some, but not about anything important. I've lied about homework, saying I'd been sick the night before and couldn't do it, when actually I'd gone to the movies. And sometimes I lied to Mom, saying something she bought was pretty because I didn't want to hurt her feelings. But those lies didn't affect anyone's life.

Mom didn't know, no one knew, how much I had been thinking about Robert Grey. I tried to imagine what he looked like. I thought of him as good-looking, tall and slim, with thick, black hair and probably a moustache. Something like the men in the cigarette ads. I don't know why but I always thought of him wearing a sport shirt and sweater and corduroy slacks. There were so many times when, out of the blue, I'd think about him and wonder what he was doing at that very moment. When I was sitting in the auditorium during graduation, I looked at the other fathers and wished that he had been there. Or sometimes when I was sick I'd lie in bed and imagine he was thinking of me.

Thinking about José Avillar made me nervous. Somewhere in my mind I knew that I was going to go to see him, and that scared me. He wasn't in Saudi Arabia, he was just a few hours from where I lived. I could get on a bus and go up to Margaret's house and see him. It was too easy. All these years I had been thinking of a search, of a long and expensive trip, of having to wait till I got older. Now I didn't have to wait at all. I really wanted to see his picture, but I was scared of it. It was like wanting and not wanting to know what I got on an exam, or if my story had been accepted in the school paper. Until I knew, I could keep hoping for something good.

It was very cold out and I wished Peggy was home so that I could go over to her house. But she wasn't. She was at a concert. So I went to a phone booth and called up Tim. Luckily he was home, and he agreed to come down and meet me at a coffee shop.

It felt good to get inside someplace warm, and I sat in a booth and waited for him. I was sure glad to see him, and, as usual, thought Peggy was crazy to call him homely. No one with that smile could be homely.

We ordered melted cheese sandwiches and milk shakes, and I talked. Tim's good about listening without interrupting, but he was wide-eyed. Every few minutes he said, "Holy cow!"

When I finished I don't think he knew what to say. "What'd you do, just walk out of the house?"

"Yeah. They're looking for the picture and my birth certificate. I feel terrible," I said. "You can't imagine what a weird feeling it is to suddenly find out a whole story about yourself you never knew before. And to have your mother lie to you about something like this."

"I can imagine. It must be awful. Like suddenly discovering you're somebody else. What are you going to do?"

"I suppose I'll go up to see Avillar. But I'm scared. I'm scared to even see his picture." I shivered, and I don't think it was from the cold milk shake.

"You want me to go with you?" Tim offered. "If you want, I will."

I wanted to hug him. "That's nice of you but I think I'd better go alone. Mom has a friend up there, maybe I can stay with her. If Mom will help me. She's angry because I'm so mad at her. It's a mess."

"She probably feels guilty. That often makes people act angry," said Tim. "What did she tell you about Avillar?"

"Not much except that he's a fisherman and he's married now and has three kids. Mom doesn't think he'd like to know that he has a grown daughter."

Tim stared at me. "That means you've got three half-brothers or sisters. Holy cow!"

The cheese sandwich stuck in my throat. I had to concentrate on not throwing up until I swallowed it. "I haven't even thought about that." I shook my head. "It's too much. What do you think I should do?"

Tim's dark face was serious. "I think you've got to see your father. Listen, I know how you feel, but don't be too mad at your mother. Grown-ups sometimes do crazy things. They can't help it. Larry's pretty decent, isn't he?"

"He's okay. Too bad she didn't marry him in the first place," I sighed.

"Yeah." Tim looked at me grimly. "They mess up their lives and take it out on us." I knew he was thinking of his own parents who had bitter quarrels that upset him. He pushed his plate away and stood up. "I gotta go. I haven't done my book report yet."

"Me either. I can't even think about it."

Tim walked me partway home. "You gonna be okay?" he asked.

"I guess so. You want a sandwich tomorrow?"

"Sure, if you've got one. Corned beef on rye, and plenty of mustard." He grinned.

"And no lettuce, I know. And thanks, Tim. Thanks for meeting me."

Don't thank me. We're friends, aren't we," he said.

Walking the rest of the way home, I decided I was ready to see what José Avillar looked like. Talking to Tim made me feel better.

Mom and Larry were upset when I got there. You'd think I'd been gone for days. "I only went for a walk," I told them.

"You should have told us," Larry said. "We were worried sick."

"Please don't do that again," Mom said. "If you want to go out just say so, but don't disappear that way. I was about to call the police."

"Okay. I'm sorry." My eyes were fastened on some photographs lying on the coffee table. "Did you find the picture?"

"Yes. Here it is." Mom picked up one of the snapshots and handed it to me. "Remember this was almost fourteen years ago. He wouldn't look like that now."

I looked at the picture of a boy in bathing trunks sitting on the edge of a dinghy pulled up on the beach. He looked like a kid. "He doesn't look like anyone's father," I said stupidly.

Mom laughed. "I told you, we were both very young. He was only twenty-two, and he looked younger."

I kept staring at the picture, hoping it would tell me something. Peggy would say he was gorgeous. But he couldn't be my father. I had always

thought that when I saw him I'd know.
I thought I'd *feel* we were related. But
I didn't feel anything. I could have been
looking at a picture in a magazine.

I handed the picture back to Mom.
And I knew I felt one thing and felt it
strongly: a new wave of resentment
against her. Why hadn't she married
him?

She was looking at me anxiously.
"So, do you feel better now that you've
seen him? You can see how young we
were. . . ."

"Yeah." I didn't want to talk to her
about him. I was angry that I didn't feel
anything, angry that my own father
was a total stranger to me. I didn't care
if she thought she had done the right
thing. I was angry with her because of
what she had done, right or wrong.

But I wasn't uncertain anymore about
what I had to do. I knew I had to see
him, and I had to see him soon.

Chapter Four

"A house divided against itself cannot stand." Abraham Lincoln said that in 1858. If that is true, our house is going to come tumbling down any day now. There's a war going on and I don't mean a little one. I am determined to go to Provincetown and Mom is determined not to let me go. Larry is somewhere in the middle. He's trying to mediate, but he's not getting anywhere.

Last night at dinner I said, "I want to go up to Provincetown to see my father."

Mom got angry right away. "You could wreck a whole family," she said.

"To put it bluntly, no man with a wife and kids wants to have an illegitimate child suddenly appear out of the blue. I wish I had never told you."

And I said, "You should have thought of that when I was born. It's not my fault you never told him. And don't tell me to forget about him. I can't and I won't. I think he has a right to know. Maybe *he'll* want to adopt me. Maybe I'll want to live with him. It's not up to you to decide."

Then Larry cut in: "But your mother's the one who brought you up. She took care of you. You owe her something."

That made me furious. "I don't owe anybody anything. None of this was my fault. Don't tell me I owe anybody anything."

Larry's remark hit Mom too. "I don't want her to feel that she owes me anything. I took care of her because I love her. You don't understand either," she said.

They ended up fighting with each other, and I felt terrible.

I didn't know how to convince Mom

that I wasn't an idiot. I told her several times that I wasn't dumb enough to go barging into José's house and announce that I was his long-lost daughter. I just wanted to find him and talk to him. I didn't know what I'd say to him. But I wanted to see him. I wanted to know what I'd feel when I saw him. I knew I'd understand a lot when I did. I'm going and they can't stop me. Last night I slept over at Peggy's and I called up the bus station and got the schedule to Provincetown. Buses go there every day. Peggy suggested I just pick up and leave. I have some money in the savings bank and I could take it out. I may have to do that, but I was scared to go and I wanted Mom to say it was okay. I didn't want to feel *all* alone. And I wanted her to call her friend Margaret and ask if I could stay with her. I didn't want to stay by myself in a motel.

Last night at Peggy's house, Dr. and Mrs. Levine asked me how I liked my new father, and I made a fool of myself. I started to cry. They thought it was because I didn't like him, and they tried to make me feel better, saying he was so nice, and that it was hard in the beginning, and I was lucky to have such a great mother and fine stepfather, blah-blah-blah. All the talk made me feel worse. I couldn't tell them the truth, and I got even madder at Mom because now she was making me lie.

I don't think it's right to lie to people about important things. Peggy and I swore that we would always tell each other the truth no matter how rotten it was. She told me she hated some of her cousins, her cousin Miriam in particular. Peggy said she's stuck-up and thought about boys all the time. I guess I have a mean streak in me because I felt good when Peggy told me that, but I didn't say that to Peggy. That wasn't a lie, it was just not saying something.

I did tell Peggy that I sometimes felt jealous of her family. She has a big family and during holidays they all come to Peggy's house. I thought they always had a good time together. But when Peggy said that their family parties were boring I was glad. You couldn't be much meaner than that. I tried to tell myself that I was glad because I wouldn't have to be jealous anymore, but I wasn't sure that was true.

Later I wondered if Peggy told me about the boring part to make me feel better because she knew how very alone I felt. Ever since Mom married Larry, I've felt more alone than before. "It's because you don't have your mother to yourself so much," Peggy said. "I used to be jealous of you—it sounded like you and your mother had such a good time together, going to the movies, eating pizza late at night. My mother and I never do things like that alone together. Either the whole family (Peggy has two brothers) goes or Mom goes with my father. She hardly ever does anything just with me."

We both thought it was funny the way we had been jealous of each other.

The night after I stayed at Peggy's, I announced at the dinner table that I was going to Provincetown. "We have mid-term vacation the end of February, and I'm going," I said.

Mom got that woebegone expression on her face and kept looking to Larry to

say something. But he simply shook his
head and kept quiet.

"Will you call Margaret and ask if I
can stay with her?" I asked Mom. "She
did invite me to come visit her."

"What would you say to José?" Mom
asked.

I could tell she was weakening. "I
don't know. I'd have to see when I got
there."

"You know how I feel about it. . . ."

"I'm not going to do anything stupid.
I promise."

"You won't mean to, but . . . Oh,
Lord, I suppose I have no right to stop
you. . . ."

"Then you will call Margaret?"

Mom looked discouraged. "You won't
give up, will you?"

"No, I won't."

"Okay. Then I guess I have to." She
put her hands on my shoulders and
studied my face. "I have to trust you,
Angela. You're going to be stepping into
a complicated and very delicate situa-
tion. Try not to hurt anyone, yourself
included. Don't expect too much. I'm

going to worry about you every minute you're gone."

"Please don't. I'll be okay, Mom. Maybe I'll just get a look at him, I don't know." But I knew I was hoping for a lot more than that.

Chapter Five

The bus station was crowded and dirty, and Mom looked anxious and kept telling me to be careful and to give her love to Margaret. "Do you want me to tell José anything if I talk to him?" I asked.

She looked horrified. "No. Just that this wasn't my idea. Be sure to keep me out of it, please. Are you going to be all right?"

I think she was more nervous than I was.

"Yes. I'll be fine. Don't worry."

"Don't expect too much, Angie." She had told me that a hundred times.

"No, I won't. Good-bye, Mom." We'd been saying good-bye for the past fifteen minutes, and I wished the bus would get started and go. Finally it did.

I took a book to read for the long trip, but I didn't open it. I wanted to think about my father. I couldn't believe that I was actually going to see him.

Then a weird thing happened. The lady sitting next to me asked me where I was going. When I told her Provincetown, she was surprised and asked me if I lived there.

"No, I'm just visiting," I told her.

"That seems a strange place to visit this time of year. I always thought of it as someplace to go in the summer."

"Well, you see, I'm going to visit my father. He lives there. He's a fisherman." It came out like I'd been saying it all my life.

"Are your parents divorced?"

"Yes. I spend my vacations with my father. There's no school this week." Our conversation made everything real. I felt like the kids I know whose parents are divorced, and who do spend vacations with their fathers. We talked more, and I told her how I sometimes went out on the fishing boat with my father, and in the summertime we had picnics on the beach and went swimming.

"You like your father a lot," she said.

"Yes, I do."

I was sorry when she got off the bus at Providence, Rhode Island. I would have liked to go on talking about things that *might* have happened. Or perhaps would happen. I knew I had lied but I didn't care. It made me feel better. I wanted the bus to speed up, not to make so many stops, to hurry up and get there.

Then I had a horrible thought: suppose my father wasn't there? Suppose he had moved away, or was out on a long fishing trip? The thought made me so nervous I ate up all the sandwiches and fruit Mom had given me for my lunch and supper. I tried to tell myself that Margaret would have told Mom if he was gone. But the idea worried me for quite a while until I fell asleep.

The bus driver woke me up at Hyannis, which was the last stop. It was very dark out, but Margaret was there to meet me. She looked exactly the same as she did in New York except that she was wearing jeans instead of a skirt.

"You okay?" she asked.

"I'm fine," I told her.

"How was the bus trip?" she asked.

"Good. I slept part of the way."

She put my bag in the back of her muddy jeep, and we drove off. I got to thinking about the lady I talked to on the bus and how easily I had lied to her. But I had enjoyed it, it had made me feel better. Now, though, thinking about it, I felt funny having made such a fuss about Mom's lying. But I still thought hers was different because it involved someone else. Maybe there are good lies and bad lies.

I was pretty sleepy so we didn't talk much, but after a short while Margaret asked me if I was hungry. I said I was starving so we stopped at a hamburger stand and ate hamburgers with fried onions. I felt better. The air smelled marvelous, salty and fresh. I wanted to ask Margaret (she said not to call her Miss Lathrop) a million questions about my father but I didn't think it was polite to do so right away. Mom said she had told Margaret why I was coming.

Margaret lived in a little frame house built over the beach. She said when the tide was high the water came up under the house, which is why it was built on stilts. The inside was just like Margaret. It was kind of plain, not much furniture, but very comfortable. There were a lot of books and pictures and she had sea shells scattered all around. There was even a fire in the fireplace.

I slept in a small room that looked out over the bay, and I could hear the water lapping against the shore and the wind blowing. I felt as if I was on a boat.

Early in the morning, bright sunshine and the crying of the sea gulls woke me up. It was beautiful out. Provincetown is a large curve of land that juts out, with the bay on the inside of the curve and sand dunes and the Atlantic Ocean on the other side. From my window I could see a long wharf with a lot of fishing boats tied up, and I wondered if one of them was José Avillar's. Maybe he was out there now getting ready to go fishing. I was afraid that I wouldn't find him, and I quickly put on my jeans and a shirt.

Margaret was in the kitchen and was surprised to see me up so early.

"I thought you'd be tired and sleep late," she said. "How about breakfast?"

"I'm not hungry now. I thought I'd go out. Is that all right?"

She gave me a funny look. "Sit down and have some breakfast. You're not going to find Avillar this morning anyway. He's out on his boat. He probably went out around four or five this morning."

"That's what I was afraid of."

"Don't worry, he'll be back late this afternoon. You'll find him down at the main wharf around five o'clock, so relax. That is, if you are still determined to see him."

"What do you mean?"

She handed me a plate of bacon and scrambled eggs and then fixed a plate for herself and sat opposite me. Her table was in an alcove facing the water, and I could see the gulls swooping down to eat.

"I'm going to be frank with you, Angela. I think I know how you feel about this, and I can sympathize, but you're making a mistake. You're not going to gain anything by seeing José, and you can do a lot of harm."

She sounded like my mother. "I'm not going to hurt anyone," I said. "I think I have a right to see him."

"Of course you have a right, but one doesn't always have to exercise a right. You're probably going to get mad at me and maybe this is none of my business, but I was involved in this from the beginning so I'm going to say what I think. You don't know the Avillar family, your mother and I do. Since she did not want to marry José or lose you, she did the right thing in not telling him about you."

"I don't see how she could have been so sure."

"Because we know José's mother."

I didn't answer. If she thought I had come all the way up here and wasn't going to see my father, she was crazy. I wasn't going to hurt anyone—and no one had any notion of what seeing him meant to me. They were playing God.

"I can't stop you from seeing him," Margaret was saying. "I can only tell you how I feel about it."

"I think you have to trust me. I'm not going to do anything stupid."

"I hope not."

Margaret told me where he lived, because the first thing I wanted to do was to see his house. She wanted me to stop at her jewelry shop, which was in front of her house on the main street, but I told her I'd see it later. I wanted to get going.

I was surprised that it wasn't cold out like New York, and although Mom had said everything would be closed in February, she was wrong. Lots of shops were open, there were people and cars on the funny narrow streets, and many of the houses looked lived-in. As I walked down the street I began to feel excited. Whether I'd get to talk to my father or not, that very afternoon I was going to see him. It was hard to believe.

I walked down Commercial Street, past the center of town and the main wharf, and every time I looked at the water and the boats I thought, My

66

father's out there. After I walked a way I came to his street and I went up a small hill. It was easy to find his house. It was big and square, white with black shutters. I stood in front of it.

Suddenly I got scared. I hadn't really thought about the house, but I hadn't expected anything so *solid*. I don't know why but I guess I'd expected something small and simple. I'd really been thinking of the young man in the picture. But this house with its white curtains at all the windows looked like it had to belong to someone much older.

I felt like turning and running away. He'd probably think I was some kind of a nut. But after a few minutes I calmed down. I wasn't going to give up. I had some crazy notion of knocking on the door and pretending I'd come to the wrong house by mistake, but I couldn't have knocked on that door if you had given me a million dollars. I just stood there hoping someone would come out and at the same time knowing I'd run like hell if someone did.

There were some bikes on the front lawn, and then three boys came around from the back of the house. Two were little, and one looked about my age but was probably younger. They were obviously brothers, probably my half-brothers. I was positive they were Avillars. So many times when I had been home alone, I'd thought how great it would be to have a sister, or even a brother. And here were these three kids, my real half-brothers, and I couldn't even talk to them.

They looked like happy kids and I thought, Sure, why not? They have a *normal* family, a *father* and a mother and brothers. They knew their father, they didn't have to wonder who he was and what he was like. I wanted to shout at them, "Your father was once in love with my mother, you jerks. And I'm his daughter. I know something about your father you'll never know."

The older boy stared at me and said hello. Lots of people in Provincetown said hello when they passed you on the street, or said good morning, so it didn't mean anything. But then one of the younger kids pointed to a house with a moving van in front of it. "Are you moving in across the street?"

"No, I'm not," I told him. "I'm just visiting."

"In that house?" he persisted.

"No, down on Commercial Street."

"I've got a new bike," he offered.

His older brother looked embarrassed. "She doesn't care about your bike."

I bent down to examine his bike. "It's very nice," I said. "Let me see you ride it."

"You're not allowed to ride it on the street," his big brother said.

"I'm going to ride it right here." The boy rode the bike up his driveway in a wobbly way and fell off. But he picked himself right up. "I went over a bump," he said, but he didn't get back on the bike.

"You were riding too slow," the older boy said, and he got on his bike and took off. I wanted to run after him, but I knew I couldn't keep up with him.

"Where's he going?" I asked.

The older of the two kids shrugged. "I

dunno. Probably down to the wharf."
Both kids turned away, obviously having lost interest in me since I wasn't
going to be their new neighbor.

I felt stupid standing on the street
watching them, and I couldn't think of
anything more to say as an excuse for
being there, so I walked away. All the
warnings Mom and Margaret had given
me were nagging at me, and I felt that
never in a million years would I be able
to let on who I was. Or even talk to my
father. I felt like a balloon with all the
air let out. But the thought of going
home and telling Mom that she was
right and I was wrong was too much.
And I knew that if I gave up now I
would *never* have a chance to meet my
father, would never know anything
about what he was like. It'd still be like
I was only half me.

I started to walk back toward the center of town. Suddenly I got mad. I could
be living in one of these houses, riding
around on a bike as much as I wanted,
having the beach right at my doorstep.
I didn't want to go home. Mom had
Larry now, and maybe I could live here.

I didn't know how, but it *might* be possible . . . I was angry all over again that Mom hadn't married José in the beginning.

Part of me wanted to stop and look in the shops, but the other part of me wanted to find that boy. Holding on to him was my only chance.

His brother had been right. He was down at the wharf, way at the end where the fishing boats came in. He was just standing there, holding his bike, watching a boat unload its fish. I had a funny feeling, watching him, that he was thinking about his father out in one of the boats, and that someday he was going to do the same thing. I wondered what he'd say if he knew his father's daughter was standing near him?

First I stayed out of his sight because I didn't want him to think I'd followed him. But that seemed dumb, so before I turned chicken I sauntered over to him, trying to act casual.

He didn't act surprised to see me.

We both watched the men weigh the fish. "They're big," I said brilliantly.

"They're beautiful," he said. I was sure he was just like his father. Imagine saying those big, dumb fish were beautiful.

I thought he was going to stand there all day. I was getting chilly and bored standing still. Finally I said, "Do you know where I can rent a bike?"

"Yeah. There are a couple of places, but one's better than the other." He started to give me directions; I must have looked confused because he said, "Oh, heck, I can take you there. I have nothing to do."

"That would be super, if that's okay with you."

He was good about waiting for me at street corners, but I ran most of the way to keep up. I rented myself a bike with four gears and then I did something I'd never done before, something I would never tell anyone about either, not even Peggy. I told Joe—that was his name— that I was nervous about riding trails alone in a strange place and since he had said he had nothing to do would he mind coming with me. I don't know where I got the nerve, but I didn't want to lose him. It was like he was my connection to my father and, in a way, to me.

He didn't seem to mind, and off we went, me following him into a bike trail. It wasn't the greatest place for conversation because most of the time we had to ride single file, but it was peaceful. Joe told me we were in part of the National Park, and he asked me to be quiet (which was a joke since I'd hardly said a word) so we would see the birds. He knew a lot about nature and was a bit of a show-off, but I didn't mind because it was interesting. I kept trying to work out a plan to meet my father, but I could only think of stupid things like breaking a leg or fainting in front of their house.

Finally I asked him if his father was out in a fishing boat, and when he said yes, I asked when the boats came in.

"He'll probably come in around five or six o'clock," he said.

"Do you go down to meet him?"

"Sometimes."

"I've never seen fishing boats come in," I said hopefully.

73

"Nothing much to see," said Joe.

"I thought it would be interesting."

"Just a dirty old boat and a lot of fish. There are dune rides at sunset. You'd like that better."

"They're just for tourists, aren't they?"

"You're a tourist, aren't you?"

"I don't like to do ordinary things," I said.

"Why'd you come up here now anyhow? Most people come here in the summer. Do you live in New York?"

"Yes, I do. What's wrong with that?" I demanded when he made a face.

"I wouldn't like it," he said.

"How do you know? You've never lived there."

"You couldn't pay me to live there."

"Nobody's offering."

We rode the rest of the way in silence. When we came to the end of the trail I wasn't even certain I wanted to meet his father. But then Joe looked at me and said, "I'm sorry if I hurt your feelings."

"You didn't. But why do people up here think New York's so terrible."

He shrugged. "I dunno. My grandmother says New Yorkers are spoiling Provincetown. But I guess she only means some of them."

"I hope you don't think I'm one of them. I like it here."

"You're okay," he said.

We rode back to the center of town and I left him to go find Margaret in her shop.

Chapter Six

Margaret wasn't keen on going with me, but I begged her to. She closed the shop at four o'clock anyway, so there was no real reason why she couldn't go down to the wharf with me when the fishing boats came in.

"I don't want any part of this," Margaret said.

"I'm not asking you to do anything except walk down there with me. That's all."

She didn't believe me and I wasn't exactly telling the truth either. If she was there with me when José Avillar came in, she could introduce me to him. But I wasn't going to tell her that now. Besides I was nervous and I didn't want to go alone.

Finally she agreed. She hadn't wanted to go and she kept muttering that neither one of us should go, but then she made me put on clean clothes and brush my hair. I teased her, and she said, "If you insist on meeting your father you may as well look your best." Before we left the house she stared at me like she hadn't seen me before. Then she said, "No one will have to tell him who you are. You look exactly like him."

Her saying that made me feel good. I don't know why but the fact that I looked like him made him seem close— if two people looked so much alike it would seem they would have to like each other. That might not be logical but that's how it struck me.

It was almost dark when we went outside. The wharf was lit up and busy with loading trucks and boats coming in. Joe and his brothers were standing with some other boys. Joe nodded but didn't come over to talk. They were right in front of a boat that was just pulling in, and I knew it had to be my father's.

I took hold of Margaret's arm, and the minute I saw José I recognized him. I knew it was him. He was so busy with his catch that he didn't even say hello to his kids. I felt very strange. Like I knew him and I didn't. It was weird. I almost wanted to cry. I felt that he was very distant, not someone you could be easy and friendly with. He was hauling fish out and throwing them up to be weighed, and he didn't look at another thing.

I held on to Margaret and I had all I could do not to cry. I don't know why. Margaret said later it was probably just the strain of being so anxious to see him, but I think it was more than that. I felt left out. I forgot that he didn't know about me. I guess I thought that he'd know. Without anyone saying anything, he'd just know.

"How long do you want to wait here?" Margaret asked.

"I don't know. Can't we stay longer?"

"I suppose so," she said. "It's your party."

"This is stupid. I wish I could meet him," I whispered.

"If he comes off the boat I'll introduce you," said Margaret.

"He's never going to get finished with those fish," I mumbled.

"That's his livelihood. He needs a good catch."

"Is he poor? His house looked nice to me."

"No, he does all right. But the fish haven't been running too well lately. This is a good haul for him."

"That's good."

I was beginning to wish he hadn't caught so many fish. It was getting cold and nothing was happening. Then he finally came off the boat. He greeted his boys and said hello to Margaret. He would have turned away immediately, but she said, "I want you to meet a friend of mine. José, this is Angela Dunoway. You knew her mother when she stayed with me one summer many years ago."

"Yes, sure. How do you do, Angela." He put out his hand and we shook hands. Then he looked at me. He seemed in a hurry but he tried to be polite. If he felt anything at all about me he sure didn't show it. "I remember your mother well. Are you having a nice visit here?"

"Very nice."

"Good. You're wise to come in the winter when it's not so crowded and Margaret has time to show you around."

"One of your boys took her on the bike trail this afternoon," Margaret said.

He looked surprised. "That's good. Well, I guess I'd better get going. . . ." He turned to his sons and they went off together.

I felt totally let down. Nothing had been the way I'd imagined. "I wish I hadn't met him," I said.

"I don't want to say I told you so, but why do you feel that way?" she asked.

"It was so flat. Nothing happened."

"What did you expect, for heaven's sake?"

"I don't know. He didn't even react to

my name. You would think he'd wonder why my mother and I still had her maiden name."

"He probably will. He's not dumb. I think he'll figure it out. But don't expect anything. I doubt he'll do anything about it."

"You mean he'll just ignore me?" Again I had the feeling that Mom and Margaret were right and that I was wrong: I shouldn't have come up. Meeting him this way would be worse than not knowing him at all. I felt as if I had been tied up and gagged—I couldn't say anything or do anything to make him know me.

Slowly we walked back to Margaret's house, and in the dark I could feel the tears rolling down my cheeks. I could never make any contact with this man who smiled and looked at me and knew nothing. I didn't believe Margaret, I didn't think he'd figure anything out. I would never get any closer to him.

When we got into the house, Margaret took one look at me and said, "What's the matter?"

"Nothing." And I burst into tears.

I didn't have to tell her. She knew. "You expected too much," she said, patting me soothingly. "I tried to warn you. But don't make up your mind in a hurry. Give him a chance. Since you've gone this far, don't give up now."

"But I'll never get to know him, " I wailed. "My mother should tell him, she should tell him she had his baby. . . ." I flung myself down on Margaret's sofa.

"She couldn't, not after all these years. Besides, she doesn't want to. You're the one who wants him to know. She can't do it for you."

"What can I do?" I sat up and wiped my face with a tissue.

"I don't know. Let me think about it."

Neither one of us ate much supper, nor did we talk much. Margaret looked preoccupied, and I didn't want to interrupt her thoughts.

After supper, when the dishes were cleared away, Margaret said, "I've been thinking. I was supposed to go to Boston this week but I cancelled it because you were coming. Tomorrow I could tell José I had to go to Boston and ask if you could spend the day with his kids since you have already spent some time with Joe. That would give you a day at his house."

"Margaret, would you? That would be wonderful. Do you think he'd be suspicious?"

"He wouldn't think anything of it. Everyone does things for everyone else around here. People make friends quickly in Provincetown. It's that kind of a place."

"Margaret, you're fantastic. Call him, please call him."

"Take it easy. I'm against this, but I guess there's no stopping you. But tell me one thing, why do you need to be with him? Why is it so important? You know what he looks like."

I didn't answer her right away. I wanted to say it right, although I wasn't sure I could because I don't know how to put all my feelings into words. All I know was that I wanted a chance to get to know him, at least a little bit. I wanted to see his house, to see what he was like in it. My mom often said you never knew anything from a catalogue or a brochure, you've got to see it yourself. I guess that's how I felt about my father. I wanted to see him as he was, more than just saying hello. I tried to tell this to Margaret. I'm not sure she understood and I probably sounded confused, but she did call up the Avillars and ask if I could spend the next day with them. I felt nervous when the answer was yes. But there it was.

I'm not going to give up now. I won't, I won't. I was sitting in the Avillars' kitchen feeling like a bump on a log. Joe had gone off on his bike, the younger boys were playing outside, and my father was nowhere in sight. Later I found out that he was down at the wharf working on his boat. I was with his wife and his mother, my stepmother and grandmother, at a kitchen table peeling potatoes for a Portuguese soup. If it wasn't so awful it would have been funny.

All night long I'd been thinking of all the things I'd say to José and how, very cleverly, without saying it outright, I'd let him know who I was, and how he would be so happy to know he had this rather nice daughter. But I hadn't even seen him, and as far as these women were concerned I was a nuisance.

I wasn't good at peeling potatoes, I took too much of the potato off, and I hated it. "Here's another bag you can do." Old Mrs. Avillar stuck more potatoes under my nose.

"All these for a soup?" I couldn't believe it.

The younger one laughed. "We're making some to freeze. You don't have to do them if you don't want to."

"Why shouldn't she? Got nothing better to do," said the grandmother. "Bet at home you get waited on. Good for you to do some work."

"I'm used to working," I said. "I know how to cook and clean and do lots of things."

I don't think she believed me. "You from New York?" she asked.

"Yes."

"Hmmph." She sniffed. I wondered what she would hink if she knew her own granddaughter was sitting in her kitchen. I wanted to tell her the truth but I didn't dare. I felt sorry for José's

wife. She had a little flowered teapot
that she was brewing tea in all morning, and I had a feeling it was the one
thing in the house that she owned. She
treasured that pot and wouldn't let anyone touch it.

It was a great relief when the boys
and José came home for midday dinner.
Not that it was a joyous affair. No one
talked much. The grandmother dished
out the food, and it was very good. I
tried to imagine my mother sitting at
this big kitchen table, but I couldn't.
Maybe it would have been different if
she had been there—she was nothing
like José's wife. Mrs. Avillar was pretty
but very quiet, and all she cared about
were the boys, especially the little ones.
She and José hardly spoke to each
other. José did attempt to make some
conversation. He asked me the usual
questions, like where I went to school
and what class I was in, stuff like that.
He didn't ask anything about Mom, but
I had this weird feeling that he knew.
I had thought it would feel right with
him, as if I belonged to him, but I felt
more like a fish out of water. A stranger.

After lunch Joe asked if I wanted to go out bike riding, and I said sure, I still had the rented bike.

He took me on another trail that was super. I liked being with Joe. I felt comfortable. He wasn't very talkative, but he knew a lot and what he had to say was interesting. He wasn't silly like some boys. I wished I could tell him that we were related, but I didn't have the nerve and I felt it wasn't right. I mean, if Margaret was right, if José really knew but wasn't going to say anything, I didn't think I could say anything to Joe. It was awful. At one point I thought I'd burst. We got off our bikes and ran up a high sand dune. When we got to the top, we looked over dunes covered with marsh grass and saw the ocean. It was quiet and beautiful, and it felt like standing on the edge of the world. There was not a soul in sight. I wanted to tell Joe who I really was, but I didn't.

On the way home, Joe said, "Let's go down to the wharf."

My father was working with another man on the boat. José came over and asked if I'd had a nice day and when was Margaret coming home. I told him she'd be back for supper.

"Am I going out with you tomorrow?" Joe asked.

"I told you yes. But you're going to have to get up early."

"That's okay," Joe said.

Then José looked at me. "Do you want to come out on the fishing boat with us tomorrow?"

I nearly fell off the dock. "I'd love it."

"Have you ever been fishing?"

I told him I hadn't. "You won't get sick, will you? It can get pretty rough," he said.

"No. I've been on boats. I'll be okay."

"Good. Meet us here at six o'clock. And wear something warm. We'll have lunch for you."

"Thank you. Thank you very much."

I couldn't believe it. It was so unexpected. He asked me, just like that. If I hadn't come down to the wharf with Joe it never would have happened.

Margaret came home soon after I got back. She was tired but she wanted to know all about my day. I told her it hadn't been anything much, except for the bike ride and then the invitation for the fishing trip.

"That means something, doesn't it, that he invited me out on the boat?" I asked.

"I wouldn't count on it," Margaret said. "He could have invited you because you're visiting and he's taking Joe. But even if he knows who you are, don't expect him to take you in his arms. First of all, that's not his style, and to be perfectly frank, Angela, even if he were faced with it directly, he might deny it. José's not about to mess up his life. Besides, he may not feel anything."

"He'd have to feel something. Can people just have babies and not care about them?"

"Yes, they can," said Margaret. "Plenty of people do. Especially when they don't bring them up, don't see them. Look at all the babies given away for adoption—for God's sake, wake up. Just because José had an affair with your mother thirteen or fourteen years ago, that does not mean he's going to love you. He doesn't even know you."

"I don't believe you," I yelled. "I'm not going to believe you. He's not a monster. I'm his flesh and blood. I'm as much his as Joe and his other kids. He can't just ignore me. I don't want to spoil his life. I just want him to know he's my father. I need him." I burst into tears. "If he were dead it would be different, but he's not. He's alive, and he doesn't even know that I exist."

Margaret held me and tried to comfort me. "I do understand. I know how hard it is for you, but sometimes there are things in this world we can't have. Not everything can always be made right. You may have to face the fact that you cannot have your father."

"I'm not going to yet. I'm not giving up."

Margaret tried to cheer me up, telling me about her day in Boston, but I wasn't very responsive. Finally she said, "Would you like to call your mother?" That was the last thing I wanted, and I told her so. Margaret laughed, but she said, "Don't be hard on her."

I went to bed right after supper. The

thought of going out on the boat the next day had lost its excitement. I almost dreaded it because I felt it would be my last chance with José. There would either be a breakthrough or there wouldn't.

Chapter Seven

Margaret insisted on getting up and giving me breakfast although I could have made it myself. She was exhausted from the day before. I was excited and nervous. "Listen," Margaret said, "have a good time today. Try to forget who José is. Just enjoy yourself. You've never been fishing before and it will be fun."

I didn't say anything. It was crazy to think for a minute I could forget who José was. I could hardly think of anything else.

Everyone was already there, busy

loading the boat. José and Joe stopped what they were doing to greet me. I asked if I could help but José said no. So I sat and watched the sun come up and kept telling myself that the very thing I had said to the lady on the bus was true. I was going out on a fishing boat with my father. Just like any other kid, I thought. Like Joe. I wondered what would happen if I called him "Dad" the way Joe did. If it just slipped out.

We finally got started and headed out of the bay to the open sea. We traveled maybe for two hours and were out of sight of land when the men threw out the seines and Joe said we'd be trolling. Joe said they'd probably get haddock and flounder.

I felt terrific. It was going to be different from the day before when he was around only part of the time. But it was agonizing too, to be so near and yet so far. Margaret said we looked alike. Didn't he see it too? Whenever he looked at me I wondered what was going through his head. Didn't he feel anything? Didn't he know?

It was weird being on that boat way out in the Atlantic Ocean in the middle of winter with two people who were almost strangers and, except for Mom, my closest relatives in the world. I thought if we got shipwrecked and drowned, they'd never know. If Tim had been there he'd say, "Don't be a dope, tell them." I wanted to, but I didn't know how, and there was never the right moment. José was concentrating on nothing but the fishing, and that kept him pretty busy.

Soon I had to concentrate on not getting sick. At first it was fun to watch the side of the boat go up and down, but the waves were getting bigger and the boat was rocking. I was afraid I was going to make a fool of myself and upchuck.

Finally I couldn't hold it back. I ran down into the galley, grabbed a pail, and let go. I knew I'd be okay if the boat would stop rocking for a few minutes, but it didn't.

I felt rotten. I was ashamed of myself and still sick to my stomach, but there was nothing left inside to get rid of, which made it worse. I wished I had never come. The whole thing was stupid: wanting to meet José, thinking he'd act like a father, thinking that meeting him would be enough, would mean something important. And coming on this dumb boat.

When Joe came down to see what happened to me, I wanted to hide. "My father said you should eat something, just bread and butter and you'll feel better. And don't stay down here, come up on deck. The fresh air will make you feel better." He didn't seem surprised I was sick, and he took the pail and emptied it.

"Thanks a lot." He was being very decent.

When I went back up on deck the sun was gone and the sky was covered with dark clouds that looked ominous to me. "Is it going to storm?" I asked Joe.

"Maybe a squall."

"Will we turn back?"

"I don't think so. Won't be anything serious. We fish in the rain."

But it did more than rain. The wind came up and I was really scared. José gave me oilskins, but I was soaking wet. I wasn't sick any more but I was terrified. I thought the boat was going to be torn in two the way the waves hit it. I thought if I ever come out of this alive I'm not going to worry about who my father is. I'll go home to Mom and do whatever she tells me. Maybe God was punishing me for coming to look for José, and if that was so, it was too bad because he was punishing the other people on the boat too. I felt as if the storm was my fault. Everyone on the boat was busy fastening things down, everyone had something to do except me.

The storm didn't let up, and I was glad to hear José say that we weren't far from Nantucket and that he was going to head in there to wait out the storm.

I was never so happy to see land in my whole life. It was beautiful to see trees and houses and good old earth looming up out of the ocean. José was very clever at maneuvering the boat to the dock and I felt a queer sense of pride watching him. That was my

father, moving so quickly and grace-
fully like a dancer, hurling ropes, and
giving orders to the other men. I had a
funny sensation, like I wanted him to
love me, I wanted him to look at me and
really see me. Before I had wanted him
to recognize me, but this was different.
It was a strong feeling, not just a
thought.

Peggy said that she read somewhere
that girls our age often fell in love with
their fathers. She said they called it an
adolescent infatuation. We had both
laughed about it and thought it was
silly. We couldn't imagine falling in
love with any of the fathers we knew.
But there, landing that boat in that
storm, I knew what they meant. The
rain was still coming down and the
wind was blowing and there I was,
dripping wet, looking at this man and
thinking I could have been someone in
his life. He was different from the fathers I knew in their business suits talking about things I didn't understand,
but I thought I understood why José
loved the ocean and fishing and boats.

As soon as we got off the boat we ran

for a restaurant on the wharf. It wasn't a fancy place, but it was warm and dry and the food was good. José tried to telephone Margaret to tell her we were okay and we'd be home late, but the phone wasn't working.

I felt snug with the storm still blowing outside, and I was hoping we'd stay overnight. The man who owned the restaurant was also a fisherman and he sat at the table with us. I was getting sleepy listening to them talk about fishing and the storm, and wished I could curl up someplace, when all of a sudden I heard something that woke me up. The man asked José if he wanted a place for his kids to sleep. José said no, that we'd be leaving when the storm slackened, and he corrected the man. He said that the boy was his son but the girl was a friend. The restaurant man laughed and said, "Are you sure? She sure looks like you." José laughed too but didn't say anything more.

But the man wouldn't let it drop. He leaned over to José and whispered, "We all could have a couple of bastards running around, couldn't we?"

"Shut up, Frank," said José.

I felt as if I had been slapped in the face. I had never really thought of myself as a bastard, an illegitimate child. I felt cold in that room that a few minutes before had felt snug and cozy. If only José had done something, put his arm around me. But his face closed up the way it had when he first saw me down at the wharf. It was as if he was seeing me but didn't want to.

At that moment I hated him. I wished I'd drowned in the storm. It was as if all the worst things I'd thought the night Mom told me about my real father, about José, came true. As if a cloud had been ripped away and I saw it all for the first time.

I sat up in my chair with my arms around myself to keep from shivering. "What's the matter?" José asked.

"Nothing," I said. "Nothing."

By early evening the storm did let up, and José said we would leave. I was glad to get going. Sitting there listening to the men talk was boring.

We had to wake up Joe and he seemed to be half asleep getting on the boat. As soon as we boarded, he went down to the galley and went right back to sleep. I stayed up on deck with the men. It was hard to believe that there had been such a storm. A few stars were showing and the wind had died down. The sea was not exactly like a lake but it wasn't nearly as rough as it had been. José gave me some blankets and a poncho, and I made myself comfortable on the deck. It was marvelous to lie there and look up at the sky. By this time I rather liked the rocking of the boat; it was pleasant, like being on a swing.

I decided not to think about anything. There was nothing good to think about, so what was the use? I often made up wonderful things that might happen, like being a tennis star or winning a lottery for a million dollars or becoming an actress, but I couldn't think of anything that night that was good. I must have fallen asleep because suddenly I woke up. I looked around and José was standing by the rail. He was looking out at the sea. Without any special thought in my head I wrapped a blanket around me and went over and stood by him.

"You're not sleepy either," he said in a soft voice.

"I just woke up. It's beautiful now, so quiet. It makes you think."

"What are you thinking about?" José turned his head so he could see my face.

"I don't know. Things. It's funny to be out here with you and Joe, when you knew my mother once."

"Karen Dunoway. That was a long time ago. How is she?" Then he hesitated for a moment. "But she must be married now with a different name. . . ."

"She still calls herself Dunoway in business. I'm Dunoway too. Kind of, that is. She just got married at Christmas. Her married name is Brandon. She's fine." I kept looking at him, waiting to hear what he would say.

"Have you any brothers or sisters?" he asked.

"No."

"Do you mind?"

"No. I'm used to being alone. Mom

always worked and . . ." I stopped for a second and then I blurted out, "I never had a father. That is, a father that I knew."

He turned away and looked out to sea again. He seemed to be silent for a long time. Then he said, "How old are you?"

"I'll be thirteen in May."

He was silent again, and I knew that he had to know. He had to. My heart was thumping under that blanket until I thought it would jump out of my body. I held the blanket close, waiting for a sign. He had to do something.

Finally he said, "But you have a step-father now. That must be nice for you. Do you like him?"

"He's okay. He wants to adopt me."

"That's good. That should make you happy."

"I told him I didn't want him to." I held the blanket closer. I was afraid I was going to cry. "I don't really need a father," I said.

Then he touched me for the first time. He put his hand over mine on the rail. "Of course you don't need a father. You're a very independent young girl.

And I don't need a daughter, much as I might like to have one." His voice was very gentle and he held my hand tight. "I have my sons. If your stepfather is a good man, and I'm sure he is, accept him. You'll be glad, and I imagine you'll make him and your mother very happy. Sometimes we have to take what we get in this world, we can't always choose. Do you understand what I'm saying?"

I wanted to pull my hand away, but I didn't. I mumbled yes, that I did understand.

When he looked at me his face was unhappy. "I hope you're not sorry you came up here. You and I can be friends, you know." He said it like he was talking to someone maybe five years old . . . like if you're a good girl we'll go to the zoo tomorrow . . . but his dark face was very upset.

"Yes, sure," I said. I took my hand away to blow my nose. I didn't really have to blow my nose but I wanted to get away.

"I guess you'd better try to get some sleep," he said.

"Yeah."

Suddenly he bent down and kissed me on the forehead. "You're a fine girl," he said. "Good night."

He turned away and went up to the front of the boat. I went back to my place on the rear deck. I was still shivering even after I'd wrapped myself in about three more blankets. I buried my head in them and closed my eyes. I didn't cry. I just felt so cold I thought I'd never be warm again. It was all over. I had found my father and I was never going to be his daughter—or even his friend.

Chapter Eight

Lying in bed in Margaret's house the next day, I was still shivering. "I think you have a fever," she said. "I shouldn't have let you go out on that boat this time of year."

"I don't have a fever. I'm okay."

"Then what is the matter with you? You're not okay."

"I am. Nothing's the matter."

"The house is warm and you're lying here freezing. Don't tell me there's nothing wrong. Did anything happen between you and José?" Margaret was standing over me with a worried look on her face. She'd been giving me hot tea and broth all morning, but all I wanted was to be left alone.

"No," I lied.

"I don't believe you. I know you don't want to talk, but I think you should. You're upset, and if you're not sick now, you will be. Tell me what happened."

"Nothing, really." I turned my face away and looked at the wall. It had pretty wallpaper with sea shells and sea creatures on it. "He knows who I am," I mumbled. "But he doesn't want a daughter. He doesn't give a hoot about me."

Margaret sat down on the bed. "Angela, darling, you knew all the time it had to be this way. He can't have a daughter now, no matter what he wants. It would be impossible. I know you had to find that out for yourself, but deep down you knew. I'm sure you knew."

I turned around and faced her. "I didn't know. Why should I have known? I thought parents loved their kids, I thought they didn't want to hurt them.

I thought my father would be glad to meet me. I didn't think he'd act like I was just anybody."

"I don't care how he acted," said Margaret. "I bet he feels as much as you do. But that doesn't mean he can do anything about it. Life isn't something that's all orderly and neat, arranged the *right* way. Things don't always turn out the way we want them to. But at least you know who he is. That's what you wanted, isn't it?"

"I guess so." I felt so tired. "But I guess I wanted more. . . ."

"Sure. You wanted him to fulfill some dream that you had. But it was not real. You made up something in your head and now you're angry that it didn't turn out that way. I sympathize, but you have your mother and Larry. You don't really need José. Not any more than he needs you. Your lives are worlds apart."

"But he's my *father*."

"By accident. You grew up fine without a father. Of course it's nice to have two parents, but it's not a disaster to have only one. People are born with

115

worse things than that. Much worse. You have one terrific parent, but you don't even value her."

"I did until she lied to me. I'll never forgive her for that."

"That will be pretty sad and stupid if it's true. You don't even begin to understand what your mother did. The courage it took for her to raise you alone, not to tell your father, not to lean on anyone. To work and to bring you up the way she did. A mother like that is a lot more than the two parents dozens of kids have. I think you're very lucky."

"Okay, so I'm lucky." I turned back to the wall again. "But she didn't have lie to me."

"Maybe she did. You kids make judgments more rigidly than anyone else. You have rules in your heads about how the world should behave, and when it doesn't you get mad. You think you're open and free, but my God, you're more intolerant than old conservatives. At least when it comes to parents. If they behave differently from the way you want, you can't stand it."

I didn't say anything. I was angry,

116

but her words were hitting home. I kept thinking about José. He was not going to acknowledge me, yet I wasn't sorry I had met him. Margaret was right when she said I had to find out for myself.

I stayed in bed that whole day, not doing anything. I half slept and half thought, and watched the gulls flying and the tide come in and then go out. Margaret went to the shop, and I liked being alone. It was a funny day. Part of me thought I wasn't going to be a kid anymore. And yet there were other moments when I thought I was never going to grow up. That I'd always feel little and alone and long for something or someone that I didn't have and would never have. But maybe that was part of growing up. I didn't know. Could be growing up wasn't only all the things I thought about, falling in love and making money and having a wonderful job and going on trips, doing what I wanted to do. Maybe it had a bad side too, like being disappointed and expecting things that didn't happen and *not* being able to do everything you wanted. Finally I decided it was dumb to worry about growing up—it would happen whether I liked it or not.

The next morning when I got up a funny thing happened. It was a lovely day and the first thing I thought was, I can do anything I want today. I didn't have to see Joe or José. I didn't have to worry about meeting José, about letting him know I was his daughter. I was free. And it was a crazy, wonderful relief.

Margaret looked worried at breakfast. "What are you going to do today?"

"I don't know. Maybe just walk around. Look at the stores, walk on the beach."

"You won't be too lonesome?"

"No. I think I'll have a good time."

She looked pleased. "Good girl."

I had a lovely time. I hadn't spent any of the money Mom had given me except for the bike, and I bought myself a pair of earrings and I bought Larry a belt, and Mom and Margaret each pretty little pottery bowls. I walked everywhere, but I didn't go down to the main wharf.

I was walking back to Margaret's shop when I met Joe. "Hi," he said. "Wanna go bike riding tomorrow?"

I thought for a minute. "No, thanks. I'm going home." I'd made up my mind just then and there.

"Oh. So long."

And he was off. So long, half-brother, I said to myself. You go your way and I'll go mine.

When I told Margaret I was going home the next day she looked disappointed. "I thought you'd stay for the weekend."

"I'd like to, but I think I want to go home."

She gave me a long look. "If that's what you want, I'm glad for you," she said.

The bus ride home was boring but it did give me time to think. I'd been mad at Mom so much I wondered if I was over it. It was the lying that had gotten me the angriest. But then I had done my share of lying too. And had it been a lie when José said he could be my friend when he knew he was in truth my father? Is a half-truth a lie? It was very complicated, and I decided that all lies were not alike, and more important than the lie was the reason for doing it. I guess Mom thought she had a good reason.

I wished I had flown home. I wanted to be back where I knew where I was, and who I was. Angela Dunoway. Karen Dunoway's daughter. But mainly Angela. Margaret had said it that morning before I left. "You're a person, Angela. A person in your own right. You're responsible for what you are and what you do. No one else. Not your mother, nor your father, nor your friends. Just hang on to that."

Mom and Larry were both at the bus terminal to meet me. I was glad to see them. Honestly glad, without needing to put on an act. And suddenly it didn't matter if Larry wanted to adopt me. If it made them happy I didn't care. It was just a bunch of legal stuff anyway because no one had a claim on the real me, the real Angela.

It took Mom until dinnertime to ask, "How did it go, Angie?"

I looked her straight in the eye and

said, "Fine. I like him, but I can hardly think of him as my father."

She looked stunned. Then she said, "You've grown up. I don't know whether to be glad or sorry."

She kept looking at me as if she expected an answer. But I had no answer for her. If she thought I had grown up that was okay with me. Could be she was right.

ABOUT THE AUTHOR

HILA COLMAN was born and raised in New York City. She attended Radcliffe College. She began writing books for young people after writing stories and articles for magazines. Ms. Colman has written numerous books for young readers stemming from her interest in the problems of adolescents. She has two sons, both of whom are married. In Ms. Colman's opinion, "The teenager has vitality and enjoys life although he sees the ugliness and absurdities as well as the joys." Among her many popular titles are *Claudia, Where Are You?*, *Diary of a Frantic Kid Sister* and *Nobody Has to Be a Kid Forever*, which are available in Archway Paperback editions.

GROWING UP...
You Can't Run Away
from It and
You Don't Have To!

29982 HIDING $1.75
Norma Klein
Krii, shy and withdrawn, copes by "hiding"—until she meets Jonathan, who helps her come out of her shell. "Tremendous appeal."—West Coast Review of Books

42062 FIND A STRANGER, SAY GOODBYE $1.95
Lois Lowry
Natalie is haunted by a missing link in her life—the identity of her real mother—so she sets out on a journey to find her. "A beautifully crafted story which defines the characters with a full range of feelings and emotions."—Signal

56042 THE CHEESE STANDS ALONE $1.75
Marjorie M. Prince
Daisy takes a stand for independence as she begins to see herself in sharper focus through the eyes of the intriguing man who paints her portrait. "Absorbing."   —Publishers Weekly

56071 CLAUDIA, WHERE ARE YOU? $1.75
Hila Colman
*Claudia feels suffocated by her family, and runs away to New York City to find some kind of meaning in her life. "...presents a thought-provoking view of a current social problem."
                                        —English Journal*

29945 LETTER PERFECT $1.50
Charles P. Crawford
*The story of three friends caught up in a blackmailing scheme. "Hard-hitting portrait of teenagers in crisis."
                                        —Publishers Weekly*

41304 THE RUNAWAY'S DIARY $1.75
Marilyn Harris
Fifteen-year-old Cat is on the road—in search of herself. "Believable and involving." —A.L.A. Booklist

41674 GROWING UP IN A HURRY $1.75
Winifred Madison
*Karen discovers she is pregnant and must make a painful decision. "A hard-hitting and brilliantly written novel."
                                        —Publishers Weekly*

ARCHWAY PAPERBACKS from Pocket Books

The Hopes, the Fears, the Problems of the Young... Jeannette Eyerly Understands Them